With much love to my incredible in-laws!
Rob and Morag, Lewis and Elena
and my bonnie niece Sofia
~ CS

For Elise, Tobias and
Amelia, with much love
~ ML

First published in 2012 by Scholastic Children's Books
Euston House, 24 Eversholt Street
London NW1 1DB
a division of Scholastic Ltd
www.scholastic.co.uk
London ~ New York ~ Toronto ~ Sydney ~ Auckland
Mexico City ~ New Delhi ~ Hong Kong

PING!

By Chae Strathie

Illustrated by Marion Lindsay

SCHOLASTIC

Once there was a funny thing,
A purple thing,
A thing with wings.
It lived with lots of other things.
Things just like him
That all went,

"**PING!**"

One day the thing was rather bored.
(Being small and quite ignored.)

He wanted life to have some **zing**.
So off he fluttered, whooping,

"Pi-inng!"

He found his way to Evie's house,

And sneaked in,
Quiet as a mouse.

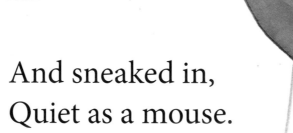

But Evie saw the little thing
And picked him up.

The thing squealed,

"Ping!"

She showed her mum
The little chap.
But Thing was scared,
Got in a flap.

To Evie's head
the thing did cling.

"There, there!" she soothed.
Thing trembled,

"P-p-p-ping!"

Evie took the thing to school.
All her friends said, "Wow! That's cool."

The music teacher said, "Let's sing –
That new boy, too." So Thing trilled,

"PI-I-ING!"

In dance class, after school was done,
Miss Tutu spied the purple one.

Thing leaped as if his legs were springs.
She cried, "Bravo!"
Thing curtsied,

"Ping!"

Evie took the thing to play.
He put on such a grand display
Of acrobatics on the swings.

He whirled and spun,
And giggled,

"Pingggg!"

At bedtime Evie said goodnight,
Lay down her head, turned out the light.

Thing folded up his tiny wings,
Fell fast asleep, and snoozled,

"Pi-i-ing."

But late one night, Thing couldn't sleep.

He tossed and turned
And counted sheep…

Once more his head
was full of ZING!

So up he jumped
And hooted,

"PING!"

And then as Evie snored in bed…

The thing went to explore the shed.

He got all tangled up in string!
Thing needed help.
He cried out,

"PIIINNGG!!!"

From all around came purple things,
Fluttering their purple wings,
Led there by the King of Things
Who sighed at Thing.
Poor Thing squeaked,

"Ping."

Thing knew that it was time to fly,
So he and Evie said goodbye.
She kissed a rather tearful Thing,

He hugged her tight
And whispered,

"Ping."

Although quite sad to see him go,

One thing that only
Evie knows…

Is any time she calls out "ping!"
A thing appears, a thing called…

PING!